THE TWELVE TERRORS
OF CHRISTMAS

THE TWELVE
TERRORS OF
CHRISTMAS

John Updike

Drawings by
Edward Gorey

Pomegranate

PORTLAND, OREGON

Published by Pomegranate Communications, Inc.
19018 NE Portal Way, Portland, OR 97230
800-227-1428   www.pomegranate.com

John Updike's text was originally published in *The New Yorker* as "The
Twelve Terrors of Christmas" under the rubric "Shouts and Murmurs."

First edition: December 1993, Gotham Book Mart, New York
First trade edition: December 1994, Gotham Book Mart, New York
This revised edition: 2006, Pomegranate Communications, Inc.

Pomegranate Item No. A128
ISBN: 978-0-7649-3710-1

Printed in China
28 27 26 25 24 23 22 21 20 19   24 23 22 21 20 19 18 17

1. SANTA: THE MAN

Loose-fitting nylon beard, fake optical twinkle, cheap red suit, funny rummy smell when you sit on his lap. If he's such a big shot, why is he drawing unemployment for eleven months of the year? Something scary and off-key about him, like one of those Stephen King clowns.

2. SANTA: THE CONCEPT

Why would anybody halfway normal want to live at the North Pole on a bunch of shifting ice floes? Or stay up all night flying around the sky distributing presents to children of doubtful deservingness? There is a point where altruism becomes sick. Or else a sinister cover-up for an international scam. A man of no plausible address, with no apparent source for his considerable wealth, comes down the chimney after mid-night while decent, law-abiding citizens are snug in their beds—is this not, at the least, cause for alarm?

3. SANTA'S HELPERS

Again, what is *really* going on? Why do these purported elves submit to sweatshop conditions in what must be one of the gloomiest climates in the world, unless they are getting something out of it at our expense? Underclass masochism one day, bloody rebellion the next. The rat-a-tat-tat of tiny hammers may be just the beginning.

4. O TANNENBAUM

Suppose it topples over under its
weight of bomb-shaped baubles?
Suppose it harbors wood-borers
which will migrate to the furniture?
There is something ghastly about
a tree—its look of many-limbed
paralysis, its shaggy and conscience-
less aplomb—encountered in the
open, let alone in the living room.
At night, you can hear it rustling
and slurping water out of the bucket.

5. TINY REINDEER

Hooves that cut through roof
shingles like linoleum knives.
Unstable flight patterns suggesting
to at least one observer "dry leaves
that before the wild hurricane fly."
Fur possibly laden with disease-
bearing ticks.

6. ELECTROCUTION

It's not just the frayed strings of
lights any more, or the corroded
transformer of the plucky little
Lionel. It's all those battery packs,
those electronic games, those built-in
dictionaries, those robots a-sizzle
with artificial intelligence. Even
the tinsel tingles this year. And isn't
it somehow terrible, the way shed
tinsel shivers in the gloomy ice-
clogged gutters?

7. THE CAROLS

They boom and chime from the
vaulted ceilings of supermarkets
and discount malls—and yet the
spirits keep sinking. Have our
hearts grown so terribly heavy,
since childhood? What has
happened to us? Why don't they
ever play our favorites? What *were*
our favorites? Tum-de-tum-tum,
angels on high, something
something, sky.

8. THE SPECIALS

Was Charlie Brown's voice always so plaintive and grating? Did Bing Crosby always have that little pot belly, and walk with his toes out? Wasn't that Danny Kaye / Fred Astaire / Jimmy Stewart / Grinch a card? Is Vera-Ellen still alive? Isn't there something else on, like wrestling or *Easter Parade*?

9. FEAR OF NOT GIVING ENOUGH

Leads to dizziness in shopping malls,
foot fractures on speeded-up escalators,
thumb and wrist sprain in the course
of package manipulation, eye and facial
injuries in carton-crowded buses, and
fluttering sensations of disorientation
and imminent impoverishment.

10. FEAR OF NOT RECEIVING ENOUGH

Leads to anxious scanning of UPS deliveries and to identity crisis on Christmas morning, as the piles of rumpled wrapping paper and emptied boxes mount higher around every chair but your own. Three dull neckties and a pair of flannel-lined work gloves—is this really how they see you?

11. FEAR OF RETURNS

The embarrassments, the unseemly
haggling. The lost receipts. The
allegations of damaged goods.
The humiliating descent into
mercantilism's boiler room.

12. THE DARK

Oh, how early it comes now! How
creepy and green in the gills
everyone looks, scrabbling along
in drab winter wraps by the
phosphorous light of department-
store windows full of Styrofoam
snow, mockups of a factitious 1890,
and beige mannequins posed with
false jauntiness in plaid bathrobes.
Is this Hell, or just an upturn in
consumer confidence?